MW01234183

A Piece Of My Mind

By Gavin Prinsloo

ISBN: 9798507431090

Dedication

I dedicate this book to two people that stood by me over the last year, though thick and thin.

Lindsay Obermeyer, the most supportive and patient of partners.

My Aunt Freda Breen – Turner, without whom I would not have survived to publish this book.

Blessed Poetry

I will start off the day, with a piece you may know,

Even if never read, its theme I will show.

It about living, in light and in dark,

It is about breathing, every moments spark.

We tend to forget, in our personal strife,

That dark we may be, but poetry is the stuff of life!

With every word, we ponder so pure,

We strengthen our hearts, life to endure.

Never give up, even though the words falter,

Lay them down soft, on the Eternal alter.

Today take a moment, look up at the sky,

Take a deep breath and for once, don't ask why.

Be Blessed.

Table of Contents

A Beggars Revenge

Standing alone, unclothed, and naked,

I stand before my Maker, humility forced from a life of the best,

He gazes down at my supine form, and challenges me,

As I lie there undressed.

"If you can answer a question for me, what did you do in your time,

That I gave you on Earth, with your life so Divine?"

I ponder the question, I answer, with pride in my voice,

" I did everything you asked of me, I kept all the Law,

I did only good out of Choice.

I did no evil, I prayed to On High,

I did my Devotions, I obeyed all your Words,

I did no one harm, not with word or a sigh,

I kept the Faith to reach my Heaven,

With my Maker on high."

The silence is deafening, a mighty Voice still, as He thought through

my answer,

And his reply was chill.

" I see that you have done all that you say,

Impressive to all to be sure, but you have forgotten ONE DAY"!

My shock is so real, it runs down my spine,

A truth on its way, a powerful jolt,

A Truth so Divine.

I wish I could bolt.

" There was a day when a beggar approached, asking for alms in need,

When away you drew, your space so encroached,

That you flinched from his touch, disgusted indeed."

" I was that beggar, in Heart and in Soul,

My purpose Divine to Judge you ahead of your time,

I sought out compassion, for a second to be whole,

For alms to be out of the ice and the rime."

" You Judged me that day, a condemnation so strong,

You brushed me off, like a flea on a dog,

You gave me no quarter, I did not belong,

To an acceptable creed and condemned me to the cold and the fog".

That day became clear, a long time ago,

I was approached by a beggar, for alms he did ask,

He stank of urine and feces, and I advised him so.

The smell of his liquor, not fresh from a flask,

Came from his pores as a robber of breath with no mask.

I pushed him away, and fall well he did,

Cringing away, crawling on all fours,

Under a bench he hid.

I took no notice, I went my way,

Nothing to give, no alms for the weak,

Nothing at all, no good to say,

Walking with head high, not a word to speak.

My Maker gave time for this to sink,

Sweat beaded my brow, fear in my heart,

And he replied, without pause or blink.

" All good you have done, be that as it may,

But one day's failure, a blow to my heart,

One day in a lifetime, no matter what you say,

Has damned you, right from the start,

For harm to me and mine you must pay."

" You are not judged by the things that please, and seem right to do,

You are judged for your love, for a heart that sees,

You are blind, Heaven is not for you."

And so, it is, with heavy a heart, and a cruel twist of fate

I missed my salvation, I repented too late.

A Breaking Dawn

I rise upon a soughing wind, my strength seems sapped,

The nighttime sleep has tired me, my soul is tapped.

I rise upon a howling wind, a howling tempestuous might,

Then looking out the window, and all my fears take flight.

I see the glow ahead, a horizon golden yellow,

I can feel my mood lifting, it now starting to mellow.

The sun breaks free of chain, the light bursts forth in blaze,

The glow of life in everything, does my eyes amaze!

The shadows they do lift and clear, bleeding into dark,

The sunshine brings alive color and form, leaving its bright mark.

Rays of life strike my eyes, I feel all life returning,

My heart beats to a different rhythm, now for life is yearning.

Now that I will endure, with pulse and heat will stay,

The pleasure of renewal takes my breath away!

A Clown in Hell

Once a year on Valentine's Day, a demon is released from Hell,

If you have never heard of this, the legend I will tell.

His name is Digby, he is a Clown,

For his evil nature, he has Hells renown.

Digby was a gentle soul, back when he was mortal,

Before his nature changed and dragged into Hells hot portal.

He pranced and danced, and he did the faces,

To goers of the circus, in so many far-off places.

For years he went along, happy as can be, performing in the ring, he was totally free.

Digby had a secret though, he had a secret crush,

On the ringmaster's daughter, in her presence he would blush.

So, one day he took a rose, wanting to declare, His love for this damsel, for she was very fair.

He told her that he loved her, and offered her the rose,

She laughed and scorned him publicly, stepping on his toes.

His huge feet a flapping, jumping up and down,

All the people laughing, at this stupid clown.

Something snapped in his heart, his soul became black as coal,

Digby was a clown no more; he became a leering ghoul.

He took up axe and knife, slaughtering all those near,

People ran around the tent, screaming in terrified fear.

A hundred souls he reaped that night, with tickets straight to hell,

Dripping blood and crushed red rose, he into evil fell.

The Devil took this creature, clown without a soul,

No longer of this earth, and with a single goal.

So be careful if you go to the circus, on a Valentine's day,

For if that clown should find you there, you will never get away.

A Consummation

As life passes, and everything speeds by,
There is only one thing I see, that catches my eye.
I see your aura green as a tree, an elemental sign calling to me.
My power of water, as blue and clean as sky,
Raining from tumultuous cloud, passing me by.

I rush to the raindrops, I impregnate with my being,
I rush through the air, the sensation is freeing.
As I hit the surface, some drops to the ground,
My being released, and floating around.

I can feel you call, a beckoning cry,
For water to give life, your skin is so dry.
Eventually I find you, I settle on leaf,
Defying dehydrations demise, I cancel your grief.

Our two elementals combining, a relationship pure,
That for ages to come, will still endure.
I wrap my wet arms around you at last, a blanket of moisture so
cool,
Reviving parched life, with the drought so cruel.

Then we envelope, our age old lovers game

Melding one into the other, it's always the same .

My essence is yours, I give it again and again,

So the Earth and Water, can make love in the rain.

A Feathers Journey

Floating on a puff of air, iridescent shine of feather gleaming in the bright light, gently rocking from dizzy height, directionless, no wing to call its own, no longer a part of a living whole, discarded flotsam in the journey of life.

Yet, in its singularity, in its moment in time where color and form caught the eye, it was whole, a singular purpose to display beauty without purpose, a momentary flash of color and beauty against a cloud filled sky.

As it floated down, cushioned by the breeze, not knowing its direction, not knowing its fate beyond this moment, its purpose was as clear as where the birds flocking into the distant horizon.

Its purpose was to have no purpose, to be beauty.

Sometimes, we need to be the feather.

A Heart of Golden Thoughts

Should color be the sound of light, and hold my heart in golden glow, cupped hands aglow, a beating golden heart with light spilling between laced fingers, laying bare the thoughts of infinite hues, a wealth of mind reflected in shafts of incandescent gleam, so bright as to narrow the eyes of perception, and shutter the window to the soul.

Sound heard without hearing, light seen without seeing, sensation felt without touching, it infuses flesh and mind, gifting the immortality of thought without thinking.

For all that is, all that ever will be, is the golden glow of life, of a heart suppurating and spilling over with the emotional heat of existence, irradiated with the promise of life.

So, as I return my heart into its suppository of self, as the light is quenched and internalized, as eyes yet see again, ears respond to the beat of my heart, and mind relax with the certainty of my temperance, my hands feel yet again the coarse texture of reality.

So again, is hidden my golden treasure, until time again to expose my mind to the light of a

beating, pulsing heart, to recreate this moment of experienced infinity, and to glow again with creativity of life.

A Karmic Thought

Stopping to talk to people, sitting in the street,

Many of them the type, that you would not like to meet.

Each one has a story, each one has their cross,

All they have in common, is each one suffered loss.

A loss of love or job, a loss of the will to strive,

Each one of them sitting there, are struggling to stay alive.

The gift of life is granted, for most it is a must,

For these souls sitting there, they have a lack of trust.

You cannot blame them for it, do not judge them hard,

Just like you and me, life has dealt their card.

Do not say that they are trash, for really people are cruel,

They really are just like us, as a rule.

We walk past them every day, invisible to our eyes,

We hear their begging and calling, and their pain filled cries.

That one was a doctor, that one he did law,

Now life has them groveling, on a dirty floor.

One thing to remember, as you walk past and do not see,

Under the worst circumstance, that could be you or me.

You are only a step away, from something that could break you too,

Now imagine if that homeless one, was you.

A Little Bit of Heaven

My head in my hands, my eyes on the floor,

I hear you come in, in through the door.

As I look up, and look into your eyes,

Ten years of life passed, where history lies.

You turn to the room, your handbag lay down,

After your work, and labor in town.

I hear you are speaking, your voice just a blur,

There is no understanding, waiting for your face to occur.

Back in the room, you still talking a storm,

Your voice light and lilting, making me warm.

' Are you listening to me, you did not hear a thing that I said',

I smile at her lightly, shaking my head.

She realizes not that a word spoken not heard,

It was not on purpose, or attention deferred.

It is life in process, so comfortable and true,

When at times I am vacant, when close to you.

As you sit next to me, I feel the heat rise,

From many years gone, but still bright in my eyes.

Our passion of body, is not what it would be,

Many years passed; of just passion we are free.

I would not trade this, some boring its true,

Not for a minute, I need more years with you.

Wealth

Mine eyes discern the beauteous hues, Mother Nature doth bring forth, upon winged rainbows she doth protest the coming of the night.

Upon her brow resplendently, she doth hold her beauty true, a tiara of light encapsulates, her eyes do shine so blue.

Glamorous glimmers she doth display, mine eyes eschew the heaven, blazing is the bounties of her light.

Upon the earth and up in sky, in tree and leaf she rides, her power in all things visible, where true beauty resides.

A New Beginning

Are these nightmares or dreams, am I awake,
Here on this mountain, I did all forsake.
How did I get here, so high up on this peak,
As I hear the wind howling, my courage is meek.

I am afraid here, shivering with cold,
My body is painful, as if I were old.
I am not waking up, so it must be real,
I bend down to touch rock, cold to my feel.

I stand again and look around, it is dark as well,
What time of night, I cannot tell.
Suddenly, a crack of light from ahead,
A gleam so bright, the darkness is shed.

The sun rises before me, it takes my breath away,
The heat replacing cold, with the onset of day.
The Suns climb majestic, climbing the ladder in the sky,
All thought is gone, and of wondering why.

My whole world encompassed, by this blazing orb,

I soak up the rays of light, joy to absorb.

However I got here, now I really do not care,

Captivated by the enormity, of a dawn so fair.

A Night of Memories

Gazing into the light rain, together arm in arm,

The evening air crisp, a calming balm,

They walked this road together, under dripping oak,

All their future, a heavy yoke.

This was their last night together, now that the war was over,

Paris had been liberated; freedom sent from Dover.

He of course a soldier, she of course a nurse,

Let us use a cliche here, to gently tender verse.

They had met a week ago, walking this same lane,

Their eyes had met, souls connected,

There the flame ignited, and their romance had affected.

To park bench and street cafe, a schnapps or two as well,

These moons struck lovers danced the dance, that we as lovers do not tell.

That week too short, soon it was farewell,

These lovers had to part, under that evenings spell.

Now many years go by, he returns now to this place,

Hoping she walks that dappled lane, his one.

last chance to see her face.

Alas it is not fate, to allow one this great prize,

to find your long-lost lover, and gaze into her eyes.

A Plague of Conscience

Looking within, my eyes turned blind,

I try to see what is in front of me, deep inside.

Who am I, what is my reason,

To be alive, in this strange season?

Strive I do, to get things right,

Always a battle, sometime frozen in fright.

What I see in my soul, does not always agree,

With the view of others, what the world wants of me.

A decision made wrong, a mistake so bad,

Impacting others, making them mad.

What is it I see, deep in my soul,

What lack of the spirit, doubting I am whole?

As days go by, and seasons do change,

All my errors compile, like a cur's sickly mange.

I try to overlook my faults, and all my transgressions,

Taking my time, in long timely sessions.

I look, and I seek,

From acts gargantuan, to meek,

I cannot separate the serious, from minor offence,

My guilt is too deep, my own judgement too dense.

I realize now, at my current age, that we are all actors, on one mighty stage.

The soaps of our lives, in many varied forms,

Determines our path, with questionable norms.

All I can say, there will be doubt,

But whatever happens, it could turn about.

A Red Rose

Deep in the night, a vision so bright,

A rose flower blooms, exuding red streaming light.

With rose in her hands, a cupped piece of magic,

The illumination bursts forth, beautifully tragic.

She has a true mission, one in ages sent,

To bring forth new life, in a rose petal bent.

Away from all eyes, all she can see,

Are small little wings, for a faery to be.

Now once a century, on this pitch night,

Is born an immortal, an incredible sight.

She opens the hands, the rose in full flower,

Out comes the Faery, an incredible power.

She places her face close, to admire the soul,

The sight is so compelling, it confounds her heart whole.

The scent is so fragrant, of life and of trees,

Also, of honey, and furry red bees.

The scent so refreshing, from a natural start,

Intoxicating light, that sets Fairy's apart.

From her hand's faery rose, just after its birth,

Light laughter soft in the air,

A flutter of mirth.

The light rises, and streaks into the wood,

To begin its existence, whether evil or good.

So it is, in next century due,

There is a faery to be born, maybe for you.

Crush not a rose, for in it could be,

Another Immortal, born to be free.

A Single Bloom

Exquisite and fine, petals like burnished silk, a single bloom in an instant of time, its image burned into the retina of appreciation, a frozen moment of pure perfection, it is beauty redolent of uncountable ages of blooms and scent.

The scent wafts across the expanse of time, it is purpose for procreation, for continuation, for abundant life, carried from generations past, each bloom a replica of the next, each flowering a confirmation of the order of the universe.

For this flower is greater than all before it, greater than the stars above, for it is born from nothing, creation repeating itself with every season, the cosmos reasserting itself and declaring itself with a tiny spectacular act of affirmation.

In the eve, petals of beauty retract to slumber, gently touched by the cool night, and reborn again into splendor with the soothing richness of first light.

Would I that this flower would never fade, that is its continued beauty be assured through the ravages of time.

Whatever my wish may be, it will fade, it will die, and serve its purpose.

That is the order of things.

So mote it be.

A Star is born

A tiny particle, its source unknown,

From somewhere in the multiverse, into this reality thrown.

Ripples spreading outward, bombarded with gamma wave,

Prior to creation, an existence craved.

Suddenly retracting, faster than speed of light,

All the ripples reversing, into the obsidian night.

Colliding neutrons glowing, the first tiny illumination,

A spark in the blackness, there can be no repudiation.

The tiny spark implodes, a universe of mass,

Forced together under impossible force, giving birth to matter and gas.

The forces too incredible, the tension cannot negate,

The blast rings through the multiverse, the mass of energy great.

Pulsing and flickering, a black hole at its core,

It begins to pull in matter, a hunger is there for more.

Again, its mass increases, the universe expands,

Then again, a mighty blast, throwing out cosmic sands.

The star we now call Sol, with its myriad string of orbs,

Now gives life to new creation, that its life absorbs

A Single Word

I remember the word in question, I knew that it was true,

The pain and confusion, the day when I lost you.

Love was just a plaster, to keep your pain away,

Now ripped off that festering wound, I know that you will not stay.

The feelings they diminished, we grew so far apart,

No one's fault really, from the very start.

The words said to each other, a verbal contract pure,

We thought our love was infinite, now we are not so sure.

Kisses and hugs we doted, the lust was strong enough,

When uttered those portentous words, the reality it got rough.

The fault is not from love, it is from that loves cocoon,

The fault is only human, I LOVE YOU way to soon.

A Tender Confusion

A plague seeks my destruction, my finger upon the pulse of redemption, my palms upon the ripe bosom of attrition, my excitement for life dampened by insecurity, and the will to survive degraded by the act of blame.

I cast my eyes upon you, from my center I am misaligned, from my mind I am disavowed.

Senses degraded by substance, my innocence corrupted by a dream without end, or a nightmare without respite.

You are there, tangible, in my confusion a focal point, in my misery my light.

Without hesitation, the disaster came rolling upon us, a ravenous maw that bit me, but thankfully left you intact.

I cast my eyes upon you, your tears a catalyst to bind me to my fate, your silence a cry in the dark, your tentative smile a blade into the softest center of my core.

I cast my eyes upon you, and for the first time I can see, I recognize the scar of the wound, the same shape as mine, a visceral reminder that though I thought you safe, I was wrong, you too were bitten,

that maw scoring flesh from bone and raking deep slices into your heart.

I cast my eyes upon you, and my heart is filled with shame, for I have no answer for your tears, love is not enough, I have no strength left,

I am weak, and you are stronger.

I cast my eyes upon you, grant me absolution for my weakness, forgive me my transgressions.

I will understand if I am too much.

Will you cast your eyes upon me?

Absolution

Falsities and fantasy, the condition is terminal,

Words spewing with no meaning, vomiting out into the world of hearing, falling on deaf ears or cold hearts.

Even the voice of Death not noticed, within the cacophony of sound, warnings of excess and indifference ignored although profound.

This continuous stream of talking, chattering through our psyche, pulling apart our sanity, and reducing us to enmity.

How can a world exist, with so much noise and sound, even Death gives up, he cannot be heard where he is meant to be found?

Mouths continually moving, the intensity of the flow, too much, too much, please let it slow!

When will the silence follow?

Nature has been supplanted, her sounds all drowned out, human noise consistent and endless, words do loudly shout.

Yet we are in a quandary, as poets we use these words, trying to make sense of the noise,

and all its hidden clues.

It is strange though that we are chosen, to fulfil this mental task, as this noise thundering in our ears, removes our human mask.

Abundancm

In these gorgeous fields of red, the soil rich with loam,

Lie the souls of many, who never went home,

Every flower a lonely soul, blooming every year,

With no loved ones to bury them, or to shed a tear.

Torn and savaged corpses, with bullet and bayonet,

Bled into this foreign soil, this beauty to beget.

By the thousands they fought and died, carrying on the fight,

To combat evil at its core, until they met their final night.

As you walk upon this land so bright, the colors a magnificent scene,

As you tread upon the blood drenched soil, feeding all the green,

Walk softly and tread careful, so as not to disturb,

The many who lay there underfoot, who the call of duty heard.

An Alternate Life

So long ago, a time of small tears,

A little boy lies awake, choking all fears.

His mind away, on its own tiny quest,

In a strange place, for some it is best.

A youth in a prison, with no iron bars,

Had a good life with clothing and cars.

At a time of his making, he steps off the world,

Where darkness lies waiting, petals unfurled.

Adventures here, a few mistakes there,

A heart free but empty, ready to tear.

Hatred keeps burning, anger a curse,

Affects all his choices, emptying life's purse.

Now sitting alone, a life near complete,

His anger all gone, hate obsolete.

The age of reason, emotion aside

The truth of it all, he can no longer hide.

No matter the cause, it is no good to hate,

Giving over to love, is a healthier fate.

Fear and aggression, that is all good and well,

But those that love, a much healthier spell.

Looking back years, a life on the run,

Missing all love, and all family's fun,

He realizes too late, those that were there.

Alectryon

A young soldier who stood guard outside the door as Ares and Aphrodite were having an illicit affair, who fell asleep on duty, and allowed Helios to catch them.

The soldier he shuffled, as he sat by the door,

Not comfortable, bored to the core.

With fidget and shuffle, his spear to align,

Protecting two Gods, both too Divine.

He listened intently, but could hear not a sound,

The darkness muffled all, with ear to the ground.

Aphrodite and Aries, a steamy affair,

Aries with muscle, she with long blond hair.

Alectryon yawned, and stretched in advance,

And shifted his body, fighting sleeps dance.

His eyes closing slowly, to sleep to submit,

He closed his eyes, sleep to admit.

Sharply awakened, with dawn in his eye,

He leapt up too late, the sun in the sky.

Helios the sun God, sees all that is revealed,

Saw Ares and Aphrodite, and their fates were sealed.

Helios ran to Hephaestus, Aphrodite's cuckold,

Who was furious, to such a betrayal behold?

A net was created, and slung far and wide,

Snaring the two together, nowhere could they hide.

The Gods all mocked them, all did scorn,

The trust broken; loyalty torn.

Aries was furious, his junior did fail,

to awake him that morning, before the reveille.

When all had calmed down, Aries did seek,

The young soldier, who now was meek.

Punishing the youngster, in a manner of the divine,

He turned him into a rooster, with plumage so fine.

Now the young rooster, forever his duty,

To call out the new day, before the sun's beauty.

An Epiphany

Drenched with blood, and diseased to the core,

The hands of the faceless, are covered in gore.

With the stench of corruption, and selfish greed,

They plant the methods of our destruction, with poisoned seed.

We feel that we have power, but nature leads the way,

Death on every street, stupidity is here to stay.

There is no way to survive, there is no going back,

Nature has passed the ultimatum; this plague will still turn black.

As the old saying goes, the one-eyed man is king,

In this world of death, that is all that he will bring.

So, go now to celebrations, as time for humanity flies,

How can we know what lies before us if our kings do not have

eyes?

An Erotic Lapse

Your skin is damp, slippery to the touch,

My fingers, sliding doing so much,

I feel your quickening, breath short on each inhale,

As my fingers spread, to gently impale.

Yours eyes rolling back, hips arching to me,

As you lay on the bed, I am setting you free.

Rocking in motion, as I massage your mound,

One hand in ecstasy, the other parts I have found.

Rubbing and tweaking, with other hand,

I bring you to your feet, you can hardly stand.

A gentle slow dance, hip swings, and gyrations,

I reach in deep, for sweet smelling libations.

My free hand exploring, every curve of your spine,

I feel your heartbeat quicken, for now you are mine.

No animal coupling, this is the game,

That gives lust its meaning and love its true name.

An Exasperating Condition of Being Human

I am not sure if I should bear my scars with pride, or take my heart from my sleeve,

After all the effort and commitment, my loves will always leave.

My soul is in commitment, my heart is yours to keep,

No matter how much I invest, I will be the one to weep.

Their love was as a bad girl, I just could not resist,

To break my heart and throw me away, I had to take the risk.

I was never a particularly good gambler, now I count the cost,

The scarring of my heart when their love was lost.

So, I accept that I am done, I loved too many and too fierce,

For the patient wait for ambush, my willing heart to pierce.

I will put my scars away now, underneath my bloodied sleeve,

To watch them walk towards the door, my heart was well received.

An Immortals Pain

From deep below, a tremor caused,

Time above, and chaos paused.

The ground did heave, the rock did split,

Stones were bouncing, an unending fit.

A fissure was formed, and out he climbed,

Not man nor mortal, undefined.

For millennia had he waited, for this day,

For his one love to come to him, and to stay.

He strode across the earth, its crust did crack,

Mountains oozing up, stack after stack.

Looking up, he could not advise,

The one thing missing, in the great skies.

So, night fell, and he wandered instead,

Lo and behold, he looked overhead.

His love was right there, high in the sky,

Her white sphere incandescent, lighting his eye.

He had longed for this moment, no explanation how long,

He had worshipped her then, with white Moon song.

Eager to touch her, he reached out his hand,

He could not reach her; on his toes he did stand.

Frustration did rip him, his fists did he shake,

He realized with pain, an obvious mistake.

The moon was too high, he could not reach,

He fell to the ground, to the heavens beseech.

The ground trembled, again it did crack,

to swallow him whole and claim him back.

Into the earth, he did return,

Gone from him now, his love she did spurn.

He sleeps on below, maybe one day to awake,

In his love throes passion, the same error to make.

Another Day Gone

Another day gone, I survived it as well,

We are all stuck, between Heaven and Hell,

Purgatories gates, open to all,

to those that rise, to others that fall.

I hope that the Demons, that chased me today,

Are gone now for good, far far away.

I try to stay true, to a heart full of good,

But every day, it burns out like wood.

Ashes to ashes, dust to dust,

Return to the night, everyone must.

For those who kept true, for those with a heart.

I thank you again, as night us do part.

When I open my eyes, may the sunshine glare,

As tomorrow, hopefully, better I will fare.

Ascension to Sublimation

Incorporeal addition to an existing abstraction,

a silent benediction, an illusion of form within a flaring conflagration.

Not smoke and flame, but an explosion of a soul's expulsion, corporeal form absolved from the strictures of the perceived reality, fealty no longer to the soft and turgid shell of need and necessity.

An expulsion of breath, a final gasp into the void of distraction, ascending to the furthest reaches of the imagination, a flash of light visible to the unknown alone, perception no longer for mortal eyes.

In an instant, from something to nothing, a smudge on the expanse of sublime silence, fading away into the womb of possibility.

The essence in the form of true self, racing ever upward into the infinite depths, an ending of a beginning, and rebirth into the end of all things.

Starlight, an impossible wink from an impossible distance, but look up into the darkest expanse, and I will twinkle for you.

For to be in existence, to be seen, to have achieved the purest form of existence, all that is needed is a flash of light, to be reborn within an explosion of silent creation.

Assimilation

Fingertips

Weapons of mass confusion

Stroking

Creating an illusion

Teasing

Rounded orbs of pure pleasure

Squeezing

Hardened tips the greatest treasure

Sliding

Southward bound a slippery mound

Cupping

Intake of breath the only sound

Parting

Lips and tongue bless moistened flower.

Probing

Fingers gently pressing more.

Slipping

A gift given with lusts full power.

Lifting

Hips raising and arched off floor.

Assimilation

Sweat reflecting hearts true course.

Acceptance

Sweet penetration with no remorse

For these moments, as time stands still,

Love not questioned, it takes its course,

Heart's desires slow to wake, hearts beating to the carnal thrill.

Aurora Borealis

A gentle static tingle in the air, gentle rays of sunshine caressing the highest cloud, a mist of gasses with fingers of silk rubbing a confluence of air, static charge created from the imagination of creation.

Taken between the palms of the Creator, gently manipulated, stretched, and enlivened with the gift of existence.

As the heat of creativity increases, a spark catches, a flare of light reaching across the prism of the expanse, a multitude of incandescent colors pleading for a chance, their existence brief, one moment alive with the glow of possibility, the next snuffed out, but reborn a moment later, roiling, boiling, earth the vessel, sun the fire.

In a state of flux, colors flickering in and out of existence, a gentle reminder of the fine line between nothing, and something, of being and not being.

Beguilement

She spins her elemental form between heaven and earth, her colors in tune with her exuded existence, fragrant with scents of life, flower petals and leaves cascading in perfumed glory, blended with the reek of sodden earth and corruption, a blend of form and scent, an alchemy of golden light spilling into the very heart of the void, birthing extensions of pulsing life into roving existence.

Her feet planted in the firmament, roots reaching for the heart of creation, anchoring the subliminal to reality.

Her hands spin the eternal loom of life, every breath and form molded in invisible hands, the only sign of the magic the winds howling into the heavens.

Clouds of incandescent color crown her countenance, her natural form not visible to the naked eye, swirling clouds laced with streaks of lightning, as her hair fans the vaults of the universe, thunder voicing her incantations, her Voice becoming form.

For She is the Mother of creation, a cycle of life reaching into eternity, and beyond.

Bittersweet Cynicism

Memories....

I like to classify my past, as either good or bad, happy, or sad.......

I think I am wrong; I am missing the point....

What if everything together is just an illusion of emotion, of a collage of finite moments.......

What if I am wrong, and all the misbegotten sadness was an excuse to cocoon myself from feeling......

If to love is to feel, and to lose is to feel, is the feeling not one and the same......

What if I am missing the chance to be really contented, my heart free from constraint and emotional affliction......

Is it in me to accept that emotions are fleeting, they do not define the inner me...?

I ask myself who I am..........

I ask myself who would love me......

I have come to the conclusion....

I ask myself why I can never truly give myself fully....

I was in love with me....

And I have lost my love......

Bleeding Words

Dripping out the corners of my eyes, drops of crimson confusion, tear drops of the deepest red, each rolling down my cheek, trails of misunderstanding and regret.

For my eyes are the window to my soul, the glass cracked and bleeding, the sparkle of Life in my eyes a crimson death, my vision obscured by lies and deceit, and certainty pouring from my mouth in a crimson tide.

Spewing hemorrhage, my tongue now stuck to the roof of my mouth, the blood concealing, clogging my airways, words pouring out from internal confusion, delayed by procrastination, jumbled by misinterpretation, and projected outward by exhalation.

There is no air, only the liquid gurgling of desperation, words drowned out and silently evicted, as my thoughts bleed out.

There is no stopping this injurious dilemma, as my soul is slowly dissolved in this deluge of internal hemorrhage, breaking off and evicted until there is nothing left but a hollow shell.

Soon, I will be bloodless, soulless, and thoughtless, eyes without sight, mouth without sound, and mind without reason.

So now I dip my pen into this crimson mess, pull close a sheet of blood-soaked parchment,

and scratch out my life essence into bleeding words, to attend to my final testament.

Broken Minds

I can hear them, they try to hide,

Their voices chiding and cajoling, like an incoming tide.

They speak of contemptable things, that my conscience cannot relate,

Controlling thought and actions, with buzzing debate.

I no longer know what is real, I have given up trying,

These voices have won, with all their screaming and crying.

I know my fears irrational, I just want to be free.

I know now there is only one voice, and that the enemy is me.

Casanova

Do not judge me by my book, or by my cover,

For I too, had my share of jealous lover.

Words are easy to speak, and to express,

Without thought or reason, while under tongues duress.

Both Adam and Eve, have had their fair share,

So many tongues throughout these times, in seedy affair.

Words to seduce, with conscience pending,

Fornicating and rutting, hearts rending.

A word in the ear, a soft inhalation,

A word of consent, a deed of damnation.

Hearing the sound, of our hearts on their tongues,

Shedding our clothing, new stockings with runs.

The real pleasure lies, in the soft-spoken word,

The wet, grinding sweat, is the cost incurred.

The words of velvet, the soft urging to partake,

Hearts do shred, and cuckholds do make.

Remember these words, while mulling it over,

Before you lay with me, Casanova.

Catoblepas

A mythical Greek figure, hairy and shaggy, with spread horns, and a face that could kill you to see, and breath that can intoxicate and kill.

Creeping in the bushes, the hunter still as stone,

Aware of the beast, he is not alone.

Ethiopia's veld, green and lush,

No sound of a bird, hoopoe, or thrush.

Then hooves sounding, vibrating the earth,

An animal so large, massive in girth.

The hunter looks over, the tall bushy stalk,

At this new danger, he cannot now balk.

He sees by the spring, the Nigris it is called,

Stands a great beast, to the water it hauled.

Not such a sight, will you ever behold,

Since the times of Pliny, the Elder, in ages old.

His foot dislodges rock, the beast turns around,

Aggressive shoulders, alert to the sound.

The big shaggy head, with giant horns broad,

Like a massive barbarian, like a forehead of sword.

Blazing mad eyes, shaggy fur blue,

Ugly as sin, akin to the gnu.

The beast it does charge, the hunter gives way,

To this ugly countenance, his feet do give sway.

All on upon him, the beast him do maul,

A sight so terrible, Marcus Aurelias would pall.

The beast he does look, straight to hunter's face,

Monstrous countenance near, and breath like a mace.

The hunter feels life ebbing, the breath it does cling,

Forcing out life's will, death it would bring.

With last of breath, and last of his power,

The hunter sees the face, that above him does tower.

His sanity gone, that vision too much,

The hunter thus screams, and his chest he does clutch.

The death rattle rolls, the monster retreat,

Back to the water, to wait for histories repeat.

Those days long gone, in the mists of time,

Remember the Catoblepas, of grasslands and rime.

He is forgotten, from all Greek tome.

I am sure he is afoot, Ethiopian fields to roam.

Changes to the Status Quo, the Last Stand

In darkest night, in sundrenched day, agony in every moment, not knowing the cause of my malaise, not accepting its origin, and rejecting all possibilities, save the cause of the affliction.

Of what I speak is disingenuous, a microscopic malignancy that shapes my every thought, every action, and grips me in a primal fear, not of Sabretooth or some other mighty beast, it is of a size unseen, obligatory handshakes and kisses to the cheek more deadly than sharpened claws or fang.

For wild beasts the spear applied, for enemies the sword, but for this malignant invader no such rendering, only an old and lonely contemplation of mortality, the expulsion of the dominant life on earth, subjugated by a callous conqueror, with no warning, no proclamation, no decree, but that of painful suffocating death.

Day after day the revolution grows, as the invader gathers strength, forever changing its form undetected, it's tactic devised by instinct to survive and promulgate, carried by countless hosts, to sow seeds of destruction at every level of existence.

Pondering on the year to come, the invader begins anew, changing form and victim, it's intent to promulgate by dissention, as none can stand before it, inciting panic, like a brush fire on a mountain side.

So, it stands back and surveys its handiwork, hand in hand with Plague and Death, a requiem hymn already hanging in the ether, the screams of dying 2021 a lamenting sound, before it is even born.

Let the bagpipes play the Last Post, as the enemy cannot be halted, but will win the Battle of the Lost, as we fall in the last charge, where arrogance, greed and blinded vision, reduce us to numberless and nameless casualties as the enemy cuts us down.

Chronos Twisting

Confluences of time, drifting, directionless, moving within the matrix of existence, the real unreal, the possible impossible, the present nonexistent.

Ever shifting, rocking within the confines of cosmic rules, yet no order from chaos, time shifting backwards and forwards, side to side, every shift a spatial anomaly, every pulse of shifted time exuding new probability, extruding the past like tendrils of smoke roiling through the clouds of combined histories and perceptions, existing within reality but only a dream in the confluence of times extinction.

A depth to the infinitely impossible, a paradox to tease the concept of the possible, the confluence streams beyond the reason of mind, beyond the concept of chronological order, no longer present as a reality, but as an enigma to tease the minds of gods.

For this is the complexity of the spark of existence, no clock ticking within the far reaches and immensity of the void, here the confluence of histories from countless civilizations meets, running its infinite loops,

no past, no present and no future exists, humanities history but a tiny irrelevant movement in the cosmic tide of time, irrelevant, and in a blink of a cosmic pulse, extinct.

Cry Not For Me

Cry not tears of sympathy when I shed my mortality,

When mine end calls forth calamity.

Let not the waters of death despoil the ledgers of my

existence,

Nor let tears fall upon its faded pages,

Let my spirit fade from life's persistence.

Ascending upon wings of dulcet melody sounding into the

ages.

Cry Not for Me.

For I no longer pledge mine breath to living word,

Within a silence of mine soul betwixt and between,

A memory of mine fortitude before mine corruption seen.

Cry Not for Me.

In memory let mine journey fade into jaded history,

That neither man nor God may judge mine obscurity,

That mine name be erased from heart and mind,

That after penance I may my final rest find.

I beg thee cry not for me.

Let mine worth be determined by loss of mine life,

May the lavish cost of time be weighed upon a smile,

Let mine peace be found within timeous extinction,

That I left mine permanence with loving distinction.

Cry Not For me, as I have already done so.

Cry Not for Me

Death and myth

Age's past, and myths do last,

Handed down, from long lost past.

Death a sequel, an existing truth,

That gives no quarter, after our youth.

So many believe, when we die,

Our essence lives on, on the fly.

Underworld and Hades, Valhalla to Heaven,

All the same destination, different names given.

What do we know, about the afterlife?

When we cannot figure out existence,

while will are still filled with life?

Death's Invisible Foe — Covid

We do not understand you; we know you are here,

We cannot ignore the fact, or that we fear.

Millennia have passed, yet still you did sleep,

Away now at last, our souls to reap.

Awful your symptoms, we do not understand,

What you have against us, so deep in the sand.

Invisible but there, we know it be true,

There is no denying, nor escaping you.

A tiny drop of liquid, an infection so vile,

That we forget the worlds troubles, just for a while.

A matter so vast, a world on its knees,

For once not threatened by winds or the seas.

We do not understand, but we do know,

That you have no mercy, like winter and snow.

Small as you are, a giant you be,

We wish you were gone, dissolved in the sea.

Yet we pause, now that understanding dawns,

That in this great battle, we are but pawns.

Nature and man, a vile combination,

We destroy what we need, without consideration.

Lessons are there, we just must learn,

that this little death, it is our turn.

It is nothing personal, this tiny mite,

It knows not, who it flattens to smite.

The world is our oyster, only now it is not,

Too much too handle, too cold or too hot.

A fever it burns, to balance the right,

But we will not go to darkness, without a fight.

Death's Gambit

In the game of life, Death always wins the game,

Or so I thought, that this night was the same.

He came to me in my dream, I was not ready to go,

I grappled with him mightily, this terminal foe.

As a result of my mettle, a grudging respect,

Death let go of my soul, a willful neglect.

He stood there and spoke, a deep bottomless voice,

He gave me a wager, a matter of choice.

If I could beat him, at a game of chess,

He would leave me alone, with no further duress.

Now few people know, Death is quite sad,

Alone gathering souls, for eons gone mad.

A wager was all he needed, to relieve his lonely existence,

His work of collection, a fatal persistence.

Now in my dream, a chessboard appeared,

A strange sight, just as I feared.

For each piece was a human soul, each in place of rank,

Now the air smelled, of decay and was dank.

So we played on, the pieces we would place,
Each piece on that board, condemned to this race.
Each time a piece taken, blood it would flow,
They would disappear in the board, going where I don't know.

Piece after piece, they fell under blade,
Screams filled the air, the last sound that they made.
Eventually I had him, my Queen the King blocked,
He shouted so with fury, that the firmament rocked.

Death had been beaten, on this bloodied board,
Dripping with blood, a sight I abhorred.

He took up his scythe, he slashed at my soul,
I felt my spirit leave me, under his control.
He stood up and pointed, skeletal finger accusing,
The loss of the game, his loss was refusing.
Even Death has his pride, his ego is great,
A powerful force, none can negate.

He chanted a verse, I did not understand,
Blue light to me sped, from out of his hand.
I felt the surge strike, I recoiled in dread,
I knew that Death always won, and now I was dead.

The story would end, were it so sure,

I woke up the next morning, soulless to endure.

My soul had been taken, so was born the walking dead,

All would now fear me, an immortal dread

Have You Ever

Have you ever stroked a moonbeam with your fingertips?

Have you ever kissed a sunbeam, with eager swollen lips?

Have you ever caught a snowflake, and caressed it with your smile?

Have you ever caught a dewdrop, and watched it linger for a while?

I would love to catch a breeze between my fingers, and braid it with a lover's touch,

I dream of catching imagination, but that would be too much.

A handful of cloud, plucked gently from the sky,

Handfuls of billowy softness, a tear sliding from my eye.

Would that I could reach up, and from the heavens pluck a star from its bed,

Rolling the shining jewel on my palm, the light shining for me instead.

Would that I could pluck the glimmer of love, a twinkle caught as it flies,

From one lover to another, before it leaves the eyes.

Would that I could stroke the moon, and cool the blazing sun,

These things I know impossible, I know that I am the dreaming one.

Though even dreams can come true, I wish these were all possible too,

To have lived in each impossible moment, until my life on earth was through.

Gods of War

Little men behind big desks, spewing a litany of ideological drivel,

Propaganda and nationalistic dogma, causing our minds to shrivel.

Leading to dictatorship, disguised as civic duty,

Crushing a countries soul, and robbing it of its beauty.

We allow these minor gods, to dictate our very existence,

Enforcing with bullet and blade, their callous and cold persistence.

These gods need to fall from Olympus, Aries needs to die,

For when he touches these small gods, there is murder in their eye.

The strangest part of all, their followers all perceive,

The words spoken in politic, who nobody should believe.

They are liars to the core, put there to rule our deaths,

Not for king and country, they rob us of our breaths.

Starting war is easy, just get someone to hate,

Until the world runs in blood, then it is too late.

So Aries smite with word and truth, so these little men can fall,

With that their castles come tumbling down, to make them again so

small.

Mine eyes have seen the glory, of the coming of the absurd,

That dost take a modern tale and twist it like a turd.

Upon the hopes of yonder futures ride, a comely inundation,

Of the tongues of mine enemies, a hellish conflagration.

It behooves me not, to sit upon thine throne,

Through worldly machinations, thy power thou did carefully hone.

Speak not to me of wealth, or fictious elocution,

Entrapped in thy cloak of wealth, a timorous illusion.

Set mine soul free, to taste creations bounty,

Free of the encumbered dolmen, invading another county.

To rid mine soul of restriction and confusing,

No more for mine pride, the morning duels are bruising.

Glory be to gods and kings, from this incumbent I withdraw,

Mine cannon set with powder, mine retaliation in mine craw.

I beseech thee now oh righteous one,

Whoever you may be,

Defuse now mine enmity, and finally set me free.

Freedoms Price

Out of a raging storm, of fire swept fury and flame,

It rose from molten depths, and from down below it came.

The spirit bird of the earth did rise, it spread it wings up high,

Flexed the heated spread of wing and ascended to the sky.

For a moment bright as day, it lit up eternal night,

All shadows chased away, seared by shining light.

Then it passed above through the skies, from west to east it flew,

From coldest night and darkness, toward the morning dew.

On and on it flew, until a horizon met,

Then flew up into highest peak, and upon this pinnacle it did set.

Raising its face into the vault of heaven, it raised its head and screamed,

An answer returned from darkest space, and a distant light it gleamed.

Fixed upon that twinkling light, it spread and flexed upon a wing,

It ascended into the sky, an ephemeral song to sing.

It took its place among the stars, it joined its cosmic kin,

It became a shining star, tonight a light to bring.

Templar

A chalice raised to my lips, red wine slipping over the brim, drops
of ruby red
like pearled blood, running down my chin, dripping onto my white
tunic,
adding a bright red stain next to the red cross emblazoned on my
chest.

The wine tart, sliding down my throat, a harsh, bitter unfermented
grape, raw,
it burns as it absolves my sins.

On my knees, bread placed upon my tongue, dissolving like acidic
flesh, I am
cleansed with the certainty of duty, to the death, and to the glory of
my order.

The Royal Arches loom above my head, keystones bearing the
weight of our
history, the cathedral dark and damp, with sconces burning with an
oily
smoke, the vaulted ceiling as black as the burnt souls of the
Damned from whom we
cleaved from flesh.

Rising, hands upon the blade guards of my broadsword, the
pommel leather
bound and cured by the blood of the Enemy, I rise to my feet, the
cold damp
of the roughhewn stone felt through the thin soles of my leather
boots and
seeping through the wrapped leggings into my cramped leg
muscles.

I stand, my armor clanging with the effort, chain mail clinking,
then silence,

my words of prayer whispered into the darkness of this holy place.

I grasp the pommel of my sword, and with a mighty roar, thews flexed with
muscle memory, swing it above my head, the shining steel whistling in the
frigid air, the combination of raw steel and the hissing promise of death,
sounding like whispering angels intent on their lethal purpose.

As blade meets flesh, rending limb from torso, and heads roll from shoulders
in a bloody spray of contrition, covering my tunic with the crimson stain of
iniquity, of the ultimate sin.

Howling with the power of the unholy possession, I cast off my helmet and
visor, my hands guiding my blade as if possessed.

Silence.

I stand in the dark, the blood of my duty flowing at my feet, stones awash
with the tide with the blood of my countrymen, of damnation I am certain.

I stand here, the last of my kind, the blood of my faith pouring down my
arms and sides, mixing with that of my brethren, mortal wounds drain me,
as I sink to my knees, sword point embedded in the stone.

As I fall, with the last of my strength, I lean my weight upon my blade, and
with an echoing crack that could be heard in Heaven, my blade snaps in
two.

As my body strikes the stone, before darkness sets in for my eternal
damnation, I rest easy in the knowledge that our legend will stand
the test
of time, and no more will our faith and duty be betrayed by Kings.

As with my sword, I break the last bonds with treachery, my duty
now only
to atone for the blood that stains my palms, feet and tunic, so
saturated,
that the crimson cross is no more, invisible, deceived by unholy
alliance of
greed and expediency.

Death greets me with a gentle hand, and with my last breath, I
surrender
myself to Judgement.

So mote it be

Goodnight

Dedicated to those with the courage to live on and are left no or little options in life.

After you read this, please look at the world differently, let empathy guide you, and judge not, in an instant, it could be you.

....
....

The concrete is cold, the air crisp, snappishly cold, penetrating old bones long used to the abuse of the elements.

A dull ache courses through his sinewy frame, a shiver felt to his core, a wracking cough released from his congested lungs, hawked into the frosted grass.

Wrapped in a dirty blanket, sitting quietly in a corner of the park under a tree, just in case it snowed, he looks up at the clear night sky, the moon bright in its eternal orbit, the stars shining like city lights viewed from the top of a hill.

He sighs, and settles back against the tree trunk, his rheumy gaze fixed on the twinkling skies, igniting lost memories, seeing faces of loves come and gone, sweet moments of completion, of happiness and contentment.

Then the recollection of the day it all changed, a moments decision, an echo of the memory that lay within the expanses of his recollection.

The memories fading away again, all he could see now was the sparkling expanse of the vaulted sky, the lights of the city answering as if in answer to the night's enquiry.

Getting colder, he hunkered further down into the blanket, alone with his conscience, but this did not bring peace and heat, but only pain.

He knew the cold was trying to force him to fall asleep, coaxing him to succumb to the rest he so dearly needed..

He had experienced many cold nights, but this night was different, the cold insistent and forcing the air from his lungs.

A single tear welled from his left eye, crystalizing almost instantly, but he could not reach up his arm to wipe it free from his wrinkled eyelid, his arms too tired to lift up for this simple chore.

He stared up again at the night sky, and he heard an owl hooting in the tree above him, then the soft silken flutter of wings faded away.

With a long, wearied sigh, he lowered his head and closed his eyes.

'Good night my love" he whispered quietly in his cracked voice, and quietly committed his history to oblivion.

Fin

Acknowledgments

A huge thank you to the Owners, Admins, Moderators and members of Dark Poetry Society, who encouraged me to publish my work, including published authors.

Steven A. North (USA)

Charles Cooper (USA),

Jimmy Kunkel (USA),

William H. Belzac (USA).

Jerry Langdon (UK),

Keith E. Sparks Jr. (USA)

The Author, Gavin Prinsloo, is a South African, residing in the beautiful city of Cape Town.

This is his first publication, he is in process of writing his second poetry book, and a novel.

Made in the USA
Columbia, SC
24 March 2022